**Here's what people have to say about the
Jannah Jewels Adventure Book Series:**

I can't continue without saying it one more time: Powerful Young Muslim Girls! No damsels in distress, no dominating male protagonist, no cliché girly nonsense! ... This is exactly what our girls need to grow up reading.
–Emma Apple, Author of best-selling 'Children's First Questions' Islamic Book Series

The Jannah Jewels books are awesome. They have made my daughters love to read with characters that dress like them and names they are familiar with. The stories keep their attention and make them curious about times past and present. We love Jannah Jewels at our house.
-Jessica Colon

The Jannah Jewels series are exactly what I would write if I had the gift of creative writing! As a mother, they are fun to read aloud as well as for the child to get immersed in! This series is the perfect blend of history, mystery, adventure and Islam! My daughter has even recommended these to her non-Muslim friends and was inspired to do a 'show and tell' on Mansa Musa thanks to these books! I'm thankful for these engaging stories and the strong female characters, thank you to the authors for a job well done, we can't wait for the rest of the series!
-Nazia Ullah

I like how you combine adventure and Islamic concepts to make us readers want to know more and more about the series. I am addicted to Jannah Jewels and I can't wait to find when and how they will get the artifact in America!
-Subhana Saad, Age 8

Fantastic book! My child was turning pages and couldn't wait to read the next chapter. So much so he's asking for the next book in the series.
-Mrs. S. A. Khanom, Book Reviewer

Our 8 year old had lost interest in reading and Jannah Jewels got her back to it. Not only that, this series has been our favourite gift to our children's friends and cousins and we hear children have a tendency to get hooked to these books!
-Umm Fatima

I have been reading Jannah Jewels for a long time and I love all the characters in this series. I can see myself in Hidayah and Iman, and I feel as if I'm in the actual story! I hope you love these books as much as I do!
-Fiza Ali, Age 10

I just wanted to thank you for these amazing books! I have 3 daughters, two of which are school age and they have recently been reading lots of Ninja Go books. We've been trying to find a better alternative for them to read and stumbled upon these, they are just wonderful! My girls are excited to read them, find them action filled and fun, while we don't need to worry about excessive violence or inappropriate language in the content. My life feels easier now thanks to these books, thank you SO much for your contribution to the Ummah, loving this series and we're looking forward to many books to come!
-Suzanne C.

My 8 year old has enjoyed these books immensely, she managed to finish each book in 2 days and has asked for more! We have made a small book club amongst our friends to swap and share the books, as mothers we love the strong role models the characters provide. We are looking forward to more books in the series!
-Falak Pasha

A captivating series with a rhythmic quest. Some of the books in the series also have surprises that made me jump into the next book right away. It's hard to put down, but at the same time I don't want to finish the book I'm reading unless there's another one waiting for me.
-Misbah Rabbani

I love all of the Jannah Jewels books, and the fact that you combine history and adventure in your stories. I also liked that you put the holy verses of Quran that remind us to stay close to Allah and I liked the fact that in one book you mentioned the verse from Quran which mentions the benefit of being kind to your enemy. I have read all of the Jannah Jewels books and even read two of these books in one day, that's how much I like these books!
–Fatima Bint Saifurrehman, Age 8

My kids liked the characters because they are modest in their mannerisms and dress, so that was something my daughter could relate to. Even though the characters are girls, it had enough excitement and the presence of supporting male characters to be read by both girls and boys. Throughout the book there was an essence of Islamic values and there was a lot of adventure to keep us guessing!
-HomeStudyMama, Book Reviewer

So inspirational... The young girls in these series are defined by the strength of their character. These non-stereotyped female role models are what our girls (& boys) need to read about. The storyline is engaging and subtly teaches moral lessons. Highly recommend these books.
-Amn, Book Reviewer

It's important for girls and boys, Muslim and not, to have strong, non-stereotyped female role models. Jannah jewels bring that in a unique way with a twist on time travel, fantasy, super heroes and factual Muslim history. It is beautifully written, engaging and an absolute must for any Muslim (and non-Muslim) kids library! My daughter LOVES The Jannah Jewels...
–Hani, Book Reviewer

We've reviewed 100s of Islamic non-fiction and fiction books from every single continent, except Antarctica, and none of the fiction books have made such an impression on our family as Jannah Jewels.
–Ponn M. Sabra, Best-selling author, AmericanMuslimMom.com

By Umm Nura

Vancouver

"To all of the young readers, dreamers, and adventurers: Stand tall and rise to bring about positive change in our world. God is with you." – U.N.

Published by Gentle Breeze Books, Vancouver, B.C., Canada

Copyright 2017 by Umm Nura
Illustrations by Clarice Menguito

Visit us on the Web! www.JannahJewels.com

ISBN:978-1-988337-03-6

March 2017

Contents

Sport:

Archery

Role:

Guides and leads the girls

Superpower:

Intense sight and
spiritual insight

Fear:

Spiders

Special Gadget:

Ancient Compass

Carries:

Bow and Arrow, Ancient
Map, Compass

Sport:

Skateboarding

Role:

Artist, Racer

Superpower:

Fast racer on foot or
skateboard

Fear:

Hunger (She's always
hungry!)

Special Gadget:

Time Travel Watch

Carries:

Skateboard, Sketchpad,
Pencil, Watch

Sport:

Horseback Riding

Role:

Walking Encyclopedia,
Horseback Rider

Superpower:

Communicates with
animals

Fear:

Heights

Special Gadget:

Book of Knowledge

Carries:

Book of Knowledge, has
horse named "Spirit"

IMAN

SARA

Sport:

Swimming

Role:

Environmentalist,
Swimmer

Superpower:

Breathes underwater for
a long time

Fear:

Drowning

Special Gadget:

Metal Ball

Carries:

Sunscreen, Water
canteen, Metal Ball

SUPPORTING CHARACTERS

JAFFAR

JASMIN

KHAN

THE JANNAH JEWELS ADVENTURE 10

INDIA

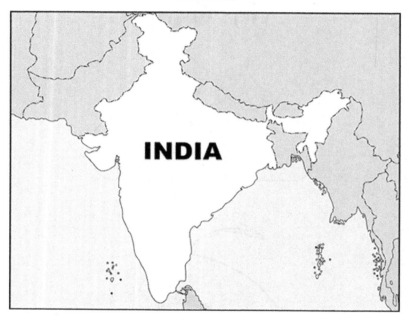

ARTIFACT 10: THE QUIVER

"We must celebrate each other's cultures to gain the wisdom Allah hopes for us. This quiver represents that diversity."
~ Sultan Razia to Hidayah

As salaamu alaikum Dear Readers,

That was a close call in Book 9: Surprise in Syria! As the Golden Clock fills up quickly with artifacts, the Jewels embark on yet another exciting and adventurous mission!

In this book, the Jannah Jewels travel back into time to India, learn valuable secrets and meet Sultan Razia who leads her people with strength and grace.

There will be a great festival taking place that teaches the Jannah Jewels how diverse people can live together in peace.

Come along, dear reader, and learn what every foundation of an empire must have in order to succeed: "We have created you from male and female and made you peoples and tribes that you may know one another."

With Warmest Salams,
Umm Nura

Prologue

Long ago, in the ancient Moroccan walled city of Fes, a decision was made. The great and peaceful Master Archer had reached old age and had to choose an apprentice to take his place and be trusted with the enormous task of protecting the world from the forces of evil. As Master Archer, he carried a deep Secret — one that no one else knew. To keep it hidden, the Secret was written upon a scroll, placed into a box and locked away in a giant Golden Clock. Who would keep this Golden Clock safe from the hands of evil after him? This decision would affect the future and balance of the world and had to be made with care and clarity.

He watched his students of archery very carefully, many of whom wanted to be chosen by their Master. Two of his students stood out to him like no other: Layla and Khan. Layla was flawless in her aim and light on her feet, who knew how to focus hard with her vision and her heart. She wanted nothing more than to bring peace into the world and use her skills in that way. Khan, on the other hand, was a fierce-fighter with strong hands and swift strategies and worked extra hard to gain his Master's attention. He had been practicing archery since he was old enough to hold a bow and learned the art from his older brother Idrees—a highly-trained senior student of the Master's.

The day finally came for the Master Archer to choose his successor and become the next Guardian of the Golden Clock and its Secret. Who would take on this great responsibility?

To everyone's surprise, he chose a woman to be the next Master Archer, the first time in history. Layla humbly accepted and continued to train relentlessly to prepare for this new role.

"Only those who are peaceful and know how to control their anger may possess the secrets of the Bow and Arrow," the Master Archer told all his students. "You must carry great humility and selflessness to lead others. Only then will you be followed."

Many of the Master's students respected and honored his decision, including Khan. He admired

Layla for her nobility and knew she must deserve this honor if the Master had chosen her over him and all the other students. Soon thereafter, he sent for her hand in marriage, and her family accepted.

The majority of the village rejoiced at their blessed union except for a few of the original Master's students. After the Master Archer announced his decision, this group of angry and disappointed students banded together and decided to leave the institution. Over time their anger turned into greed and jealousy. They spread rumors about Khan saying that he only married Layla to gain power and get his hands on the Golden Clock. They devised plans to separate the two great archers and steal the Clock along with its great Secret.

Layla and Khan were unaware of these terrible schemes. Khan went on to become a successful businessman and a leader of his community. The couple lived happily practicing the ways of the Bow and Arrow together whenever time permitted. They were blessed with two children: a boy named Jaffar and a girl named Jasmin. Jaffar was a gentle and curious spirit who loved to practice calligraphy and read as many books as he could. Jasmin was quite the opposite as she loved to play all kinds of sports, tumble and practice archery like her mother.

Khan had great expectations of his son and would push him to practice archery more. Jaffar was not a natural at it like Jasmin, nor had as much interest in it as her. To please his father, he would practice every day with Jasmin, although he just wanted to read and write. Jasmin enjoyed teaching her brother and loved being praised by her father. The family lived peacefully in their villa for some time until the day came that everything changed...

1

Mother

"Who's there?" Sensei stood up in front of the girls as if to shield them.

"Mother? Is that you?"

Jasmin stepped out of the shadows, her arm stretched out toward the girls. Her jaw dropped as she saw her mother for the first time in years. Suddenly, memories from her childhood flooded Jasmin's mind.

She could smell the steaming mint tea that her mother would pour masterfully from her shiny teapot into tiny blue glasses on sunny summer afternoons and how she would hold it up against the sunlight to check the colour. The more golden the tea, like the sweet honey that was added to each glass, the more flavourful was each glass.

She remembered how Khan, her father, would bring home bright yellow melons from the market for lunch after Jumu'ah, the Friday prayer, and Layla would cut them open and blend the sweet fruit into cool refreshing smoothies to drink.

Jasmin let the joy of seeing her mother again flood over her. She ran forward, her hijab fluttering behind her. Sensei Elle wrapped her arms around her daughter, as Jasmin collapsed into them, letting out a deep sigh.

"How I have missed you, my daughter. Every night, I prayed, in sha Allah, I would see you again and tell you how much I love you!"

"Mother, I understand now. I understand why you left. When I was younger, I was not mature enough to appreciate the duty you had to protect the secret of the Golden Clock." Jasmin consoled her mother.

Sensei rubbed her daughter's back. "Yes, my duty as the Master Archer was too important. But I am still sorry I had to leave."

"But mother, why…" Jasmin's voice trailed off.

"Yes, my daughter?"

"If you knew that the artifacts had to be collected, to protect the secret of the Golden Clock, why not send me and Jaffar? You know our skill, how hard we have worked on our skills! Why not return to our family and let us help you in your duty?"

Jasmin's lips trembled and hot tears ran from her eyes. The girls felt such empathy toward her, even though they were still afraid to completely trust her. They watched on in silence and deep thought.

Jaide promised herself she would give her mother a huge hug as soon as she returned home. She was missing her home cooking. She shifted her eyes to Sensei Elle, who looked upset. The Jannah Jewels had never seen Sensei Elle look so restless and weary.

"Oh, Jasmin! Do you not see?" Sensei Elle's voice rang with a tenderness that only a mother could speak. "The quest to retrieve the artifacts, open the Golden clock and reveal the secret is so dangerous." The Jannah Jewels shook their heads in agreement.

"The secret can not fall into just anybody's hands. It is too powerful."

Sensei continued, "There are pitfalls that I feared would be too great for you and Jaffar. Even with the four of the Jannah Jewels, some of the challenges have been so hard that it is only by Allah's guidance and His help that they have succeeded. I wanted to protect you and Jaffar. And..." Sensei Elle trailed off.

"And you already knew it had to be us," Jaide gasped, "because we met you! Or you met us! Or... we met each other. Years ago, or... minutes ago... in Aleppo... in Syria. You knew we were the right people for the mission because you met us long ago in your youth!"

Sensei nodded. "Yes. All those years ago, you told me we would meet again. For years, I wondered who you were, and how I would meet you again. But when Hidayah came to my house in Vancouver, I recognized her, and it all made sense. I knew Allah's plan, for me to train her and send her and the other Jewels on the quest."

Jasmin began to understand. "We have to follow

Allah's plan, even if we do not know where it will take us. All that matters is that He has brought us back together. And now that we all know who is trying to retrieve the artifacts, we can just return home, mother, and leave the task to the Jewels!"

Sensei's eyes widened. "No, Jasmin, you don't understand. I have a duty as the Master Archer. I must protect the secret. I must guide the Jannah Jewels in their quest."

"Jasmin," Hidayah whispered, and Jasmin turned to see her former foe. "Jasmin, why were you crying in Aleppo?"

"My father, he did not understand why you were pursuing the artifacts. When he sent Jaffar, he did not know that he was interfering with our mother's duty to protect the clock. When I attacked you all in Spain and in Turkey, I thought you were my enemy. I wanted to please my father. I…" Jasmin's voice trailed off.

"I wanted to be better than my brother," she continued after closing her eyes. "I did not listen to my heart, or Allah. And I am sorry for what I did.

And I understand why you did not trust me. I was so frustrated with myself. So I followed you through the tree, to see if I could find my mother, and to see if I could gain your trust."

Hidayah placed her hand on Jasmin's shoulder. "We have so much yet to learn, all of us, but maybe we can learn it together. Perhaps if we all work together, we can find the remaining artifacts and protect the secret. Then your mother could return to Fes with you."

Jasmin nodded her head in agreement. "We will all work together." She leaned forward and hugged Hidayah. Hidayah felt lighter in her heart. She felt forgiveness enter. She knew that if Jaffar could change, so could Jasmin, and she trusted Sensei Elle's words.

Jasmin and Hidayah turned to look at Jaide, Iman, and Sara, ready to embrace them. But when the pair turned, their faces lost their smiles.

Jaide's arms were crossed, her foot on her skateboard, pushing it back and forth. Iman looked at the ground, shuffling her feet, while she nervously

tugged at her hijab. Sara's eyes glared with anger as her hands sat on her hips and she bounced her foot impatiently.

"Hidayah," Sara said, "we need to talk."

2

Trust

Hidayah walked across the inside of the tree to where her three friends were standing. Sara stomped her foot on the dirt floor. "Are you out of your mind?"

Hidayah pursed her lips and prepared for a fight. "Sara..."

"Where do you want to start, Hidayah?" Jaide's voice was firm. "She threw ambergris at us. She fought us at every opportunity. We could have been stuck back in time or even worse, we could have been killed!"

"I understand, I'm listening..." said Hidayah.

Sara interrupted, "She attacked me, Hidayah. She stole the artifact from me in Turkey, remember?

13

She tried to stop us from protecting the Secret in the Golden Clock."

"Who knows what her plan is now?" Iman continued. "She is playing a game with us, sneaking in here! And how did she get in here anyway?"

Jaide chimed in, "We saw her in Syria. She delayed us there and we almost didn't get home! She must have followed us through the tree."

"Followed you? That must be her plan!" Sara's eyes were bright with concern.

"She didn't delay us in Syria, Jaide," Hidayah snapped back, "she gave us the artifact and helped us complete our mission."

"We can't just believe she has changed. We can't just let her be here with the Golden Clock," Iman implored. "Please, Hidayah, come to your senses!"

"She has worked against you and your Sensei since the first day! She snuck in after you!" Sara begged.

Jaide nodded excitedly and shouted, "She snuck in after us and without our permission! We can't trust her!"

"Jannah Jewels!" bellowed a voice from behind them. "I cannot believe what I am hearing!"

The girls turned around to see Sensei Elle standing with her hands on her hips. Next to her stood Master Swimmer, Master Artist, and Master Horseback Rider. The four women seemed to have a mix of frustration and concern on their faces.

Master Artist began, "Jaide, trust is something which must be earned, yes. But you must give someone an opportunity to earn that trust."

"You must forgive her for attacking you, Sara," the Master Swimmer commanded, "because she has recognized her wrongdoing and seeks change. Forgiveness is a gift from God that we can share with others."

"We have all made mistakes, and we must all mature as we learn from them. It is wrong to deny Jasmin that opportunity," Master Horseback Rider concluded.

Hidayah understood in her heart that several of the previous missions were barely successful.

Adding another skilled young woman to the team would make them all the more ready for whatever challenges were presented in finding the remaining artifacts.

"All of your skills are necessary for your next missions, even Jasmin's. You will need to trust her opinion and listen to her ideas," Master Artist argued.

"The other Masters and I do not always agree on how to complete missions. We discuss, each bringing our knowledge to the table," Master Swimmer continued, "and if we disagree, we still respect one another. We trust each other through thick and thin."

"So you must do the same. You must forgive," Master Artist said firmly, "and forget. Jasmin will work with the Jannah Jewels to obtain this next artifact. That's how it must be."

The girls nodded to each other, glancing over at Jasmin, who stood across the room, talking to her mother. She looked genuinely happy, the first time any of the Jannah Jewels saw her with a positive emotion on her face. They each felt God soften their hearts at the sight of her smile.

"Hidayah, come here," Sensei Elle motioned for her to join the mother-daughter pair. "I have a note for the two of you."

Hidayah walked over to them, while the other three Jannah Jewels chatted with their respective mentors. Sensei Elle pulled out a piece of paper and handed it to Hidayah. "This is for you to meditate on, Hidayah."

Hidayah looked down at the paper in her hand. Jasmin looked over her shoulder. On the paper, someone had written a verse from the Qur'an in beautiful flowing Arabic with the English underneath.

We have created you from male and female and made you peoples and tribes that you may know one another.

"May your reflection and contemplation provide you with a deeper understanding of God," Sensei Elle whispered solemnly.

Sensei turned to face the crowd, and raised her voice happily. "My sisters, it is time for the Jannah Jewels to go on their next mission. With each

17

artifact, the Clock grows more charged, but also more unstable. There is no time to waste before the next mission!"

"One more thing, girls," Master Swimmer called out. "Sensei Elle forgot to mention..."

"Oh, yes, of course!" Sensei Elle smiled warmly. "Where you're going, there will be a wise woman to guide you. Think of her as another sort of Master, like us. Sometimes your team must be made of many women, with different skills. Find this fellow master. She will show you her wisdom."

"We will seek her out." Hidayah felt relieved that they would have help on their next quest. "Does everyone have what they need?"

The girls each checked their pockets and bags. Hidayah had her compass and map. Jaide had her watch and both her skateboards, still carrying her old one for Mus'ab. Iman had her Book of Knowledge and her Book of Animals. And Sara had her canteen, ready in case they went back to the desert. Jasmin checked her bow and arrow, to be sure they were ready in case the Jewels got into trouble.

"Trust in Allah's plan, girls. You're going to have to all work together if you want to get this next artifact!" Sensei Elle called as the girls pushed their way through the tree trunk.

As the girls slid down into another time, Sensei Elle could hear Jasmin's voice among the chorus reciting, "Bismillah hir Rahman nir Raheem."

"Woah!" Jasmin yelled as she fell out of the tree onto the ground, hitting the damp, mossy surface hard. The other girls stepped out of the tree, and Hidayah offered her hand to Jasmin to help her to her feet.

"Don't worry, you get used to it," said Hidayah, extending her hand out, as Jasmin blushed.

3

Mangoes and Snakes

The girls looked at the tree, with its thick, sticky trunk and huge, glossy green leaves. "It's muggy," Sara noted, "like a jungle environment. We seem to be on the edge of a jungle. It's beautiful to see jungle like this in the past, before people cut them down."

"Yeah, it is beautiful, but do you think it will have bananas? Or other fruit?" Jaide asked impatiently. "We didn't stop for food since Syria and I traded away my last snack."

"Oh, Jaide, hungry again? It's like we are searching for the artifacts, and you're searching for your next meal," Iman teased, nudging Jaide gently and laughing.

"I just don't see why we can't find both at the same time? Besides, we don't even know what we're looking for or where we are!" Sara exclaimed.

"Well, we must be in the tropics if we're on the edge of a jungle," Iman noted, opening The Book of Knowledge. "It looks like that is a mango tree. Hidayah, did you bring the map?"

Hidayah reached into the sleeve of her robe. "You bet I did! Let's compare the map with what you can figure out about the climate."

Hidayah's fingers traced along the map until they came to a stop on top of some bold letters.

Artifact #10

Quiver

India, Southeast Asia

"India!" Jasmin exclaimed. "I've always wanted to go to India! I can't believe we're in India!"

Iman furrowed her brow, "Yes, but we have no idea *when!* There are many great Islamic periods in India, and I don't know how to tell *when* we are!"

Hidayah responded, "Well, the Qur'anic passage

we are supposed to reflect upon is about other tribes - maybe we should find some other people and ask them for information."

"Well, we can't go hiking off into the jungle," Iman countered as she read more about Indian jungles. "It says here there are all sorts of plants that are dangerous. And animals like tigers, and elephants. And s-s-s-nakes!"

"Please no snakes," Sara begged.

"Yes, snakes," Iman continued. "But it looks like we're on the edge, and there seems to be a path along the edge here. Maybe we should follow the path until we can find other people."

"As long as there are no snakes, I'm in," Sara voted.

"All right, ladies, let's follow the path. I count one, two, three, and me..." Hidayah looked around in a panic. "Where's... where's Jaide?"

"I'm here!" Jaide yelled.

The girls looked all around them. Jaide's skateboard was at the base of the mango tree, but she was nowhere to be seen. Suddenly, there was a loud thud, and a mango fell from the top branches of the giant tree. Another, then another, and the girls looked to the source of the half dozen flying mangoes.

"Mango delivery! I'm coming down!" Jaide yelled as she shimmied down the trunk of the tree and jumped down to the ground. "These looked tiny from down here, but when I climbed up, they smelled ripe and tasty. I picked one for each of us!"

Each girl reached down and picked up a mango. Sara stuck hers in her backpack, while the other girls each tore theirs open and began to snack.

Jaide stuck one in her backpack too, making sure it was safely packed beside her old skateboard. She picked up the extra mango, cracked it open, and began cleaning out the seeds so she could enjoy the bright, fragrant fruit.

"Wait! Why do you get a second mango?" Sara laughed and poked Jaide in her side.

"Well, did you go for the mango? No! And that climb was so tough! Are you sure you are brave

enough to man-go up the tree to get more?"

"Jaaaaaaide!" Iman groaned, "your jokes are so bad!"

"But this mango is so good! Thank you!" Jasmin chimed.

"And mangos are all biodegradable! So this is a healthy snack that is good for the environment! We can throw the mango rinds into the jungle when we're done, and animals can eat them," Sara said with great satisfaction. "You're so smart, Jaide."

"Well, let's eat and walk, ladies, because we've got a quiver to find!" Hidayah took the lead and began walking down the path along the jungle's edge. As they reached the top of a hill, they looked out ahead of them, and saw small packs and pairs of people walking ahead of them. Behind them, several groups of men and women were climbing the hill and would reach them soon.

Jaide pulled Iman up onto her skateboard. "We'll zoom ahead, and ask those people for information. You wait up here, and when those people come up the hill, you ask them *when* we are. Then we'll run back here, meet up and share."

Jaide and Iman sped off, with Sara skillfully handling the rough dirt trail while Iman held her waist for balance.

Hidayah, Sara, and Jasmin waited on the hill until the travellers behind them reached the summit. The first trio of travellers wore bright red silk robes unlike any that the girls had ever seen. On their heads, bright orange scarves were wrapped into tight headdresses.

The men each had long, curled mustaches, and were in the midst of merry conversation as they walked. The fattest of the trio seemed to laugh at nearly everything the other two said.

Hidayah summoned her courage and walked up to them with her head held high. "Salaam, gentlemen! I was wondering if you could tell me what year it is?"

The men stopped talking and looked at her, confused and amused. One began speaking to the girls, but his words seemed so foreign to them. They could not recognize a single word the men spoke. The girls shook their heads.

The fat, jolly man smiled and made a happy sounding yell. He pulled out a small paper note from his belt and unfolded it. While laughing, he held it in front of him and motioned to Jasmin to take it. She reached out and took it from him.

"What does it say, Jasmin?"

"Uh…. I… I don't know!" As the other girls looked over Jasmin's shoulders, they stared at the hand-written calligraphy on the paper. Bright flowers decorated the borders, while text of different sizes told the reader important information that the girls could not understand. Jasmin looked up at the happy man.

He smiled at her, and said a few words in a mystery language. He pointed to the paper, then pointed down the road. He bowed a bit, and the trio of men continued their walk down the other side of the hill, resuming their joyful conversation. Soon, the belly laughs of the friendly man became faint, and then disappeared.

"Let's hope the next traveller is more helpful," Sara sighed.

"In sha Allah. I will pray until the next people come. And I will pray that Jaide and Iman have more luck down there," Hidayah pointed down the hill to where Jaide and Iman were chatting with a pair of men wrapped in bright green cloaks.

Jasmin and Sara sat quietly, studying the paper. "Do you even know which side is the top?" Sara finally whispered.

Jasmin flashed a glance over to Sara, paused, then shrugged. Sara smiled, and giggled, and Jasmin giggled as well. Sara reached in her bag and pulled out her mango, and after cracking it open, offered a part to Jasmin. The pair enjoyed the fruit, as well as a few sips from Sara's canteen.

"Ladies, I need your help," Hidayah called out. They looked up to see her standing with an elderly woman wrapped in brown cloaks. Jasmin hopped up, carrying the mysterious paper with her, and Sara jogged over to join the pair.

"I can't understand her. And I don't think she sounds anything like the men," Hidayah sounded uncertain and worried. "I am so confused, because I can't understand anyone here."

The old woman began talking in a warm voice that soothed the girls. They knew she meant them no harm. But the sing-song nature of her voice was so strange, and her words were made of sounds they did not recognize. Sara shook her head while Jasmin raised her hand with the paper.

"Nimantran," the old woman cheered, "Nimantran!"

She reached up her sleeve and pulled out another brown paper, rolled tightly. She unrolled it and handed it to Hidayah, smiling and nodding. Then she reached forward and patted Sara on the shoulder gently, smiling and pointing forward along the path. She continued walking, leaving the girls speechless.

Hidayah looked down to the paper in her hand. It was covered with swirls and lines, artfully painted. She sighed and felt like a weight was resting on her shoulders.

"I don't know, my friends. I can only hope that Jaide and Iman have found more success than us..."

4

The Puzzle

"Oh man. I can only hope the other Jewels have found more success," said Iman.

Iman looked down to the paper in her hand. It was covered with swirls and lines, artfully painted too. That was the third paper she and Jaide had collected, skateboarding from traveller to traveller.

All three were similar, but the print was different and she couldn't recognize any of it.

"Jaide, let's go back. This isn't working. Maybe Hidayah has an idea." Iman walked back, head drooped, and hopped on the back of Jaide's skateboard. The two skated up the hill, taking advantage of the engines on the skateboard, until they found the other Jewels sitting in a triangle, staring at brown papers in front of them.

"This side is up," Jasmin said, "I'm sure because when the man handed it to us, he was holding this as the top... right?"

"Ohhh, good idea. And the scroll is probably rolled from bottom to top, right?" Sara guessed.

"Oh no! You guys got papers too? Did anyone speak a language you knew?" Iman was hopeful that their luck had been better.

"Nope. This is so hard! How do we find out what these say if we can't read them?" said Jasmin. "How do we even know they are related?"

"Well, look at this. All the paper is the same. It's the same color. Probably made from the same plant," Sara remarked, putting the five sheets together and weighing them in her hands.

"And they all have the same flower borders," Jaide noted, "all painted by the same hand. Someone produced all these papers in the same workshop. Then different people did the calligraphy."

"So line them up with the borders matching. Look," Hidayah said excitedly as they lay the five papers in a line. "They all have sections with different sized text. They match up."

"I bet these all say the same thing in different languages, like some kind of announcement... or an advertisement." Jasmin smiled. "So if we each take one copy and try and decipher one portion, then we can figure out what the whole thing says faster."

"Down the hill, we saw a small pond that a lot of people were resting by. We can go down, walk around until we find someone who understands the papers." Iman pointed down the hill, "it'll be faster and more effective."

The girls followed the path, each holding a sheet and studying the text. They divided it into five sections, each taking one. When they reached the clearing, Hidayah turned to the group.

"Alright, sisters. Here's the plan: you find someone who can read your paper, then get them to explain your section." Hidayah motioned playfully. "Think of it like charades! Just ask them to act it out… we have to have faith in God to help us make sense of this."

The girls each took a deep breath and began walking over to a set of travellers. Each girl walked from man to pair and woman to pack. Once each found someone who could read their paper, they sat, trying their best to translate their section through dance and action.

When Sara pointed to her section, a pair of young women began a series of dances, one like a juggler, then a singer, then an archer, then like a bird. Then one acted as if she was rewarding something to the other.

Jaide pointed to her section, and an old man acted out eating and drinking, then sat back and rubbed his belly and smiled.

Hidayah pointed to her section, and everyone she showed it to cheered, "Razia!"

Jasmin pointed to her text, and a pair of men wiped clean the dirt in front of them, then used a stick to draw a map. Jasmin nodded her head, even if she didn't know where the drawing was pointing to, because at least she knew it was a location.

As the girls came together, Iman was already leafing through her book. "My section was a date, and I've been looking in The Book of Knowledge. I think I know *when* we are!"

"So we knew we're in India. The paper says it's 1238 AD, during the Delhi Sultanate. This period of history was another Golden Age, full of art and science! Under the Sultan, people of many religions lived together in peace, and many languages were spoken throughout the land."

Sara growled, "That's why the pages were in all those different languages! We're in an empire and we didn't bring a translator!"

"This says that one of the greatest Sultans ruled during this year, a Sultan Jalalat-ud-Din Razia. It says here he ruled for four glorious years full of peace and prosperity." Iman continued.

Hidayah's ears picked up, "Razia! His name is on this paper! The people I talked to made a motion like Razia held everything in his arms. He must be the Sultan and the people love him!"

Iman finished, "it also says that the Sultan sponsored many feasts and festivals."

"Yes! Festivals with performers and awards!" Sara proclaimed.

Jaide cheered, "And feasts! I knew it! Feasts! Finally!"

"These must be invitations! My section was a location, so there must be a festival going on now!" Jasmin nodded confidently. "All these people from all over the empire are coming to see the Sultan at the festival!"

"If we follow them," she continued, "we will find our way to the festival, and maybe the Sultan will know where we can find that quiver."

"Great idea! Let's go!" Hidayah hopped up, and started down the path.

"Wait!" Iman squinted in confusion, "Something is odd about this entry. Every time Razia is called 'Sultan', it is written in a different color and underlined. Like it's different."

Jaide whined, "Iman! Not now with the book!

According to my watch, we've only got 8 hours to find this quiver, and the Sultan might be our only chance. We've got to go find him and see if he knows where the artifact is!"

The girls chased after Hidayah and the pack left the clearing, heading on the main road to a hillside. The road passed over a trickling river to a patchy bit of jungle on a mountain hillside. By now, the road was full of travellers, with sounds of music and laughter filling the air.

As they rounded the hillside, before them lay a small valley filled to the edges with crowds, tents, stages, and tables.

5

Crisscrossing Paths

"Look at all the people!" Jasmin proclaimed, and the girls stood in awe. In the huge clearing in front of them, people spilled out as far as they could see. The sound was a rowdy mix of voices, animal calls, and musical tones. Poles with bright flags marked intersections of paths, while tents and canvas sails fluttered in the breezes above.

"Praise Allah, is that a... is that a...?" Sara exclaimed in excitement.

"An elephant!" Iman responded, her heart racing at the sight of the magnificent beast in the distance.

"A festival!" Hidayah and Jasmin said in unison.

Hidayah turned in relief. "Wow, now I understand

why the flyers were in different languages! There are so many people here. The Sultan must have invited people from across all his lands, near and far, to celebrate at the festival."

"And by writing in all their languages, he makes them all feel equal and important," Iman noted, nodding. "That seems smart for a leader. This must be why my book said he was wise."

"With all these people here," Sara noted, "surely we can find the woman who is supposed to guide us that Sensei Elle mentioned back in the tree. Surely, she is here somewhere. What I am not sure about is..."

"...how to find her?" Iman finished Sara's sentence, having the same thought. The massive crowds pulsed and shifted like clouds in the sky, filling the space in front of them with energy and color.

Jasmin set her jaw. "We've got to split up. I will stay here. Each of us will go to a section of the festival, and look for the wise woman there. Then, once we find her, we come back here and find the others."

"She's right, Jewels," Hidayah agreed. "Let's each take one of the paths from here and search within it." The girls walked to the first split in the paths and separated, each praying to God that He would give her guidance.

Sara walked into an open square, each edge fringed with camels draped with heavy, woven rugs. The patterns varied from camel to camel, from ornate flowered silk rugs woven in Turkey and Persia to thick, maroon wool rugs fresh from the looms of the mountainous deserts of historic Afghanistan. In front of each camel, men bartered and yelled, trading and selling the beautiful wares.

As Sara walked on, she saw one short, squat old woman. Her purple hijab fluttered behind her, as she sat on a pair of fat silken pillows. Her hands held a needle and thread, and they moved with a dizzying speed.

As Sara watched, the woman talked to the first man in line in front of her, took a pair of pants from his hands, bent over them, and began sewing with a

great sense of purpose.

After just a few moments, the woman handed the pants back to the man, who handed her a pair of shiny coins, smiled and bowed his head, and moved along. The next man handed a pair of gloves to the woman, and received them back in exchange for a pair of starfruit.

Sara approached the woman gently, and realized that the woman was repairing tears in the men's clothing. "What a smart idea," Sara said to the woman, "and so good for the environment. Instead of throwing away clothes when they tear, you repair them. Our beloved Prophet, peace and blessings be upon him, was known to repair his clothes."

"And these men," the old woman replied, "many of them are old. Their wives have died and their daughters are married and gone."

"They come to my stall when they visit the festival, and I take care of these repairs. This small business lets me keep a small house for myself now that my husband is gone. For God knows that men and women need each other, for we all have skills that contribute to society." The woman kept sewing.

"Plus the Earth needs people to protect our resources. You are a wise woman indeed. May I help you sew?" Sara sat down and began helping the woman repair the hem on a pair of bright red trousers.

As Jaide walked, she watched singers and dancers perform along the road. But ahead of her, she noticed a small crowd gathering around a sharply dressed woman sitting on a short stool, drawing on what looked like a make-shift easel. Jaide approached, joining the side of the crowd. She set her skateboard on one end and stepped precariously on top, struggling to get a better view.

The woman was using a dark, charcoal pencil to draw on a single white paper held in place on a wooden board resting against a stump in front of her.

Jaide expected to see her writing ornate calligraphy - perhaps even making more of the invitations they had collected earlier - but as she watched, she saw the woman quickly sketch a portrait of an ornately dressed man standing in front of her. The crowd began to cheer as she drew, and Jaide understood why.

The artist painted a large nose and tiny chin on the portrait, making the face look like a cartoon. When she finished, she handed it to the muse, who had a merry chuckle while the crowd yelled again.

Another man in the crowd volunteered and paid the artist a pair of coins, and then she placed another paper on her board and began her work.

After enjoying a good laugh or two as the woman drew her portraits, Jaide yelled out, "fine artist! Why do you paint the faces with such humor, instead of drawing them as truly as possible?"

The woman did not even lift her eyes from her canvas while answering. "There are more sides to a person, my friend. Anyone can paint the side that everyone sees. But my art captures the humor of a person, because we laugh together while I draw. So I paint a different truth. We are all made of many truths."

Iman walked for a few minutes, lost in the crowds of her section at the festival. She wanted to open her book and read more about the sights around her, but she knew she could not keep her nose in the book when she was supposed to be searching around her. All of a sudden, her ears perked up at the sound of a loud screech. She turned around, and in the clearing ahead of her, some men stood with a pack of animals around them.

One man in lemon yellow pants held his arms extended like branches, with brightly colored birds of all shapes and sizes resting along them, waddling beneath them, or fluttering around him.

Just a few feet away, a man sat on a tall stool with the largest snake Iman had ever seen draped over his neck. But Iman was drawn to a young girl surrounded by a pair of ferocious lions.

Iman gasped, looking in panic that no one was stopping these lions from devouring the young girl. Yet, as Iman watched, the girl raised her hand, and the lions lay down in front of her.

This girl must be a Master of Animals, Iman realized, as the girl stepped forward, sat down next to the lion, and began rubbing its belly. The lion rolled on his back like a kitten, and blissfully let the girl rub him down.

Iman approached the girl, thinking that perhaps she was the woman Iman was seeking. Suddenly, she heard a growl, and looked over her shoulder to see a tiger prowling behind her. The crowd around them had grown silent. Iman looked to the young girl, who stopped petting the lion and called out to Iman in her tiny, angelic voice.

"A calm heart is contagious."

Iman took a deep breath, and prayed to God to calm her heart. She turned around to face the tiger, and knelt slowly to the earth. She cautiously extended her hand to the tiger, and looked into the brooding tiger's eyes with peace and calm. She remembered her Master's lessons about calming her mind and using her knowledge of cats to stay still and remain patient.

The tiger stood still, like a statue, for a second, then its tail dropped and he trotted over to Iman. He licked her hand with his giant tongue, and lay down next to her. Iman could feel the calm and peace in

the tiger, and she relaxed. She reached forward and tickled the tiger under the chin, and he began to purr.

"You see. A calm heart," the young woman called, and the crowd relaxed, resuming its various conversations.

Hidayah pulled out her compass, and prayed to God. She knew that she needed to find the wise woman the Masters had mentioned, and she needed to find her fast. She closed her eyes, and focused on the Qur'anic passage given to her for the quest, but she could not understand its deeper meanings.

After a few minutes of intense supplication to God, she felt a familiar tug in her heart, driving her forward through the crowd to a bold pink tent decorated with roses and vines. There was a small stage that hosted two men in strange robes Hidayah had never seen.

But all should work to stay on path

So that we avoid Allah's wrath

The first man proclaimed these words in a confident tone, and Hidayah realized that it must be a live poetry competition. The poet's words rang out like a song, but carried a heavy weight.

The crowd murmured and mumbled, and many shook their heads in agreement. Hidayah watched the second poet scratch his beard slowly, his mind deep in thought. With a quick motion, he raised his head.

It is better to follow Allah's rules from above

Not out of fear of his anger,

but because of your love

The crowd cheered triumphantly as the words rang out. Men and women raised their hands in applause, and the second poet took a brief bow.

Then, to the crowd's delight, a beautiful woman walked up the short ramp to the stage. She motioned to the second poet and the entire crowd went silent.

"Love is always a better motivator than hate. The poet from the Turkish lands is victorious!" Her voice was crisp and melodic, and her words were met with cheers. She walked off the stage to the side, carrying with her an air of importance.

Hidayah suspected this woman might be a clue

to where their artifact, the quiver, could be. She followed the woman out of the tent, then quickly ran up to her.

But before she could ask the woman for a moment of her time, a pair of men in light chain armor stepped in front of Hidayah. "Just who do you think you are?" the first man barked at Hidayah. "You do not belong here."

"I just wanted to ask that woman for something. Please let me through," Hidayah cried. But the second man crossed his arms firmly across his chest and blocked the way with his huge body.

"I see you have a bow and arrow. You may be a threat to the Sultan. You must leave now. If you don't leave on your own accord, you don't want to know what will happen next."

6

Sultana?

"Guards, guards! At ease!" The woman spoke with confidence and control, and the guards immediately backed away from Hidayah.

"Sultan?" Hidayah cried out in shock. Hidayah turned quickly, looking all around her. "Where? I don't see him!"

The beautiful woman tilted her head and began to laugh. "You're not from here, my sister, are you?"

Hidayah still did not understand what was happening, but she felt calmed by the woman's smooth voice. "No, no, I am not from near here. My friends and I, we have travelled from very far, and..." Hidayah trailed off as the woman's bright eyes grew wide. She smiled.

"You and your friends? You must be the Jannah Jewels! I did not think I would find you until after the feast this evening. I hope you'll dine with me at the feast so that we can discuss the item you must find. I will explain it to you all." The Sultan gestured to Hidayah to approach. "Where are your friends?"

Hidayah shook her head in dismay. "I... I don't know. You must be the wise woman we are seeking to learn from. But we didn't make a plan for what to do after one of us found you. So I do not know how to find them."

"Well, then, perhaps my good friend Haati can help! Let us see if he can lift our spirits," the Sultan exclaimed with a sweet ring to her voice, while directing Hidayah around the tent of poets. As Hidayah looked to where the Sultan gestured, her eyes travelled up the rough grey wrinkles of the elephant.

"So, that's Haati?" Hidayah asked. "Well, I've always wanted to ride an elephant."

With the help of the two guards, the Sultan was

boosted up a pole to a large silver cushion resting on the back of the elephant. She reached her arm down, and helped pull Hidayah up to her.

Then the Sultan leaned far forward and whispered into the elephant's ear. He lifted his heavy legs and began the regal walk up the path. The guards walked ahead of them, ensuring Haati did not step on any distracted revellers.

From atop Haati, Hidayah was able to see much more easily through the crowd. All around, people looked happy, and many bowed graciously at the sight of the Sultan's elephant, cheering her name. Hidayah directed Haati around the carnival, passing through each area until they found one of the Jannah Jewels.

Each time, the Sultan helped the Jewel up onto the back of Haati. Finally, they made their way to Iman, who was lounging on a rug while gently petting a massive, purring tiger.

As Iman turned to see her friends and the beautiful woman, her eyes traced the elephant's massive trunk and she smiled. "What a magnificent creature! Hidayah, who are our new friends?"

Hidayah called out from atop the elephant, "This is the Sultan, Iman! This is her elephant friend, Haati. Come up; we must ride him over to the feast!"

But Iman was looking deep into Haati's eyes and stroking his trunk gently. "No, Hidayah, Haati is upset. He says he loves to carry the Sultan, but now he has four other girls on his back. He says it is tiring, because he must also walk carefully to avoid stepping on anyone."

"Oh no!" Sara cried, "we must all get off! Haati is an Indian elephant - such a rare species! We have to protect rare animals, not use them cruelly!"

One by one, the girls hopped down with the help of the guards. Then, Sultan Razia reached down. "No wait, Sultan!" Iman raised her hand. "Haati insists you stay atop him. He says it is an honor to protect you and serve you, that it is his duty given from God to help your people see you and trust you."

The Sultan pet Haati on the head, and the girls walked along with the guard in front of the pair. As they approached a beautiful blue and green striped tent, Haati stopped and waited as the Sultan descended. They touched foreheads, and then the Sultan led the girls into the tent, which held several tables covered with maps and manuscripts.

Iman's eyes widened, and she exclaimed, "Elephants and manuscripts! Sultan! You must be a most wonderful ruler, like my book said. But…"

The Sultan laughed, "but you were expecting the Sultan to be a man, right? I understand your confusion. Before my father died, he chose me to be his successor. I have always found that I must project power like a man, even though I am a woman, so that my soldiers and guards obey me."

Sara asked, "Weren't your brothers jealous?"

"Sometimes. Other times, they recognized that I would be the best leader." The Sultan turned to Jasmin and said gently, "perhaps some of you understand the challenges of having talented brothers."

Jasmin shook her head, remembering her fight with Jaffar earlier, and the tensions between them that caused problems for her father.

"Was it difficult for your father to break from tradition and choose a woman for the throne?" Jaide asked, entranced by the beautiful Sultan.

Sultan Razia shook her head and smiled. "No. My father was a wise man who studied the Qur'an with an open mind. He could see that men and women should be equal in Islam, and so he chose the best leader for his people. Men and women both have strengths that can make them a true Master. It simply requires Muslims to be open minded and hear Allah's message of fairness and equality."

"You know," Jasmin said distantly, "my mother and father never talked much about how they had to compete to become the Master Archer. I knew they trained together growing up, but they never talked about how it felt to compete. And mother never talked about the massive responsibilities she had to take on as the Master Archer."

"Indeed. Sensei Elle," Hidayah blushed a bit calling her by a different name, "she told me many times that protecting the Golden Clock was a serious duty. She said it had cost her everything, and it required her full attention and effort. She prayed everyday to Allah for the strength to hold such a hard position."

"You must understand," Sultan Razia said, "not only is it hard to be a good leader, but not everyone believes that a woman can be a good leader. So as a woman in a powerful position, I must work even harder to be a great leader, not just a good one."

Sultan Razia turned to Jasmin, and whispered, "I'm sure your mother feels the same way."

She placed her hand on Jasmin's back reassuringly. The other girls hung their heads, feeling sadness that such a kind and brave woman like Sensei Elle had to endure such challenges just because of her gender.

Though they did not know what the others were thinking, they each said a prayer to God that each of their Masters would find peace in their role as a strong female leader.

"Let us not be sad, ladies!" Sultan Razia raised her hands above her head and clapped them twice quickly. A pair of male servants came with a large copper bowl full of steaming water and a cloth. Behind them, a young woman carried a small glass bottle.

The Sultan washed her hands in the hot water and dried them on the cloth. She then let the young woman drizzle oil on her hands, rubbing them together. Sultan Razia motioned to the girls to do the same, and they did.

As Sara raised her hands to her nose after rubbing the oil around them, she recognized the soothing scents. "Orange and mint," she exclaimed. "This reminds me of our time in Spain."

"My new friends, tonight I invite you to join me for the talent competition. Whoever I decide possesses the greatest talent shall win my silver quiver. You can help me choose a winner," the Sultan offered.

"Well, actually, Sultan Razia, we were hoping you would call off the talent competition. The quiver that is the prize is the artifact we came here for," Hidayah explained, "and so we need to take it with us."

"Oh, no, I'm sorry. But I've made a promise to

my people that there would be a talent competition and the quiver would be the prize. All are here to see it. And I cannot lie to them and just give it to you." The Sultan warned, "we must be honorable women and honorable Muslims if we wish to be worthy of our duties. So you will have to win the competition fairly if you want to take home the prize."

"But do not fear," she said with a wink and a smile, "I also know that there is more to be found in this competition than the prize. Have faith that Allah will let your true talents be tested."

"First, however, we must eat," Sultan Razia sang. "There is a feast for all to enjoy!"

"She said eat!" Jaide sprang forward. "Please show me the way to the feast! I have to practice my talents before the competition!"

Iman laughed. "Oh, sweet Jaide, what skill is that?"

Jaide replied, "Feasting! An important talent indeed! Now can we satisfy our lovely host by accepting her invitation? Please?"

The girls laughed. "Absolutely, Jaide. For once,"

Hidayah smirked, "we'll let you lead the way to the food!"

7

Reconnection

Jaffar and Khan gazed across the hillside by the Tomb of the Merenids, overlooking the city of Fes. Jaffar stood with Khan, each with an easel in front of them. The city's old walls were the subject of their paintings, with their crumbling corners requiring shades of tan and brown.

Jaffar always found painting to help him relax. Art and calligraphy had always been Jaffar's favorite pastimes. The ability to create a new perspective on Allah's creation filled him with purpose. Often, when Khan had pushed Jaffar to focus on his archery, he would sneak away at night and paint to soothe his tired hands.

Khan had never taken painting seriously. Khan assumed it was an art form only for relaxation, not to be thought of as serious study. Yet after his concussion, Khan struggled to focus and calm his mind and eyes. His doctor recommended he take up art therapy to help relieve his anxiety.

Khan and Jaffar now sat, painting together. It was new for Khan, but for the first time in many years, he felt close to his son. He felt a calm in their souls. As the brushes colored the canvases, they discussed the Qur'an and the role of faith in the construction of the beautiful, ancient city below them.

"I understand now, Jaffar," Khan said as he added a touch of blue to the brick work on his canvas. "There is a cleanness to painting. Your mind empties, and it is easier to reflect on Allah and life when your heart slows and your mind is at peace."

"I am glad you are able to find peace after your injury. I was so afraid for you father," Jaffar said. "I was afraid I would lose you like mother."

"But I grow stronger every day," Khan reassured his son. "And now that I know that your mother leads the Jannah Jewels and that we all work for the common goal of protecting the Golden Clock, my faith has been restored."

"I did not know I could trust the Jannah Jewels. In fact, I thought they were my enemy. Now, I think back on all the danger I put them in. They were working hard to protect the world, and I put them in great danger," Khan's hand lowered and he shook his head. "I hope they will someday forgive me. I hope your mother will forgive me."

"Jasmin will find the Jewels, father." Jaffar was confident. "I have spoken to them, and they understand that this has all been from confusion. Jasmin has always been the more clever one of us, so she'll figure out a way to bring everyone together. She will find them and mother and tell her that we need her back."

"My son, it may not be so simple. We must first uncover who is threatening the Golden Clock. We must win the Archery Battle; it has to be either you or Jasmin," Khan sighed. "Or one of the Jannah Jewels. But we must protect the secret inside the

Golden Clock."

"What's the big secret anyway?" Jaffar asked as he added a puffy white cloud to his canvas.

Khan laughed heartily. "Now, if we all knew what it was, would it really be a secret?" He shook his head. "I do not know. Only the Master Archer knows what the secret refers to, but even she does not know the truest nature of the secret. That is why we must work together to protect the Clock and its secret."

Both father and son continued to paint, breathing in the clean hillside air and enjoying the glorious afternoon Allah had granted them together.

Back at the house, in the kitchen, Aunt Nur sliced carrots and added them to a huge pot cooking a chicken couscous stew. Mus'ab sat with her, drinking mint tea and keeping her company.

"You've been helping to prepare for the Archery Battle? " Mus'ab asked.

"In many ways, yes," Aunt Nur replied. "For years, I have supported your Uncle Idrees. I've helped write correspondence. Just this month, I have been hand-writing the invitations and posters. My handwriting, like my sketching, is lovely, important and masterful."

"I've studied texts with Idrees, and prepared prayers. Now, I help prepare the materials: the bows and arrows, the banners and flags. A woman's work, whether as the Master Archer, or as a support for her husband, is never done."

"And a good man is nothing without a strong woman," a voice filled the room with warmth. Idrees walked in, snuck behind Nur, and stole a slice of carrot. Taking a quick bite, he smiled.

"I have always considered myself so lucky to have Nur here by my side. I feel such guilt, knowing that I had even a small part in the separation of Layla and Khan," Idrees said with regret.

"But now that Khan knows that Layla, I mean Sensei Elle, has been guiding the Jannah Jewels, they can be reunited, right?" Mus'ab said with great excitement.

Idrees and Nur looked at each other, sharing a concerned look. They alone understood the complexity of the situation at hand. Reuniting Khan and Layla would not be as easy as bringing them together. There was still an Archery Battle to decide.

"My dear, I did not come in here to discuss the Jannah Jewels," Idrees said firmly. "I came because you promised me a steaming pot of mint tea and a pretty plate of almond cookies. My brother and nephew have returned from their painting on the hillside, and you asked me to play host."

"Of course! Here is the tea and cookies, Mus'ab," she looked with mock seriousness to the boy. "You better escort these cookies in with my husband. Leave him alone with them, and all he will have for our guests is the tea and some crumbs!"

Idrees laughed, and the men left Nur to her cooking. Idrees carried the hot copper teapot and a shining tray with magenta glasses, while Mus'ab successfully guarded the cookies all the way to the living room. They sat, and Idrees began pouring tea as Jaffar and Khan continued their deep conversation.

"But father, it doesn't make sense," Jaffar insisted.

"My son, there have been shadowy forces before. When you were young, do you not remember when your mother was forced to flee?"

Jaffar sighed heavily, "Of course, father. How could I forget? But that doesn't explain anything."

Uncle Idrees cut in. "What doesn't make sense? What seems to be the problem?"

Jaffar turned to his uncle, clearly distressed. "Well, we now know that the Jewels were headed by mother, Sensei Elle, the Master Archer. That means that mother formed the Jewels and sent them out to find the artifacts because she thought they were in danger."

"Yes," Khan confirmed.

"And she thought that if the artifacts were in danger, than the Golden Clock and its secret were in danger?" Jaffar asked.

"Yes!" Khan agreed, "yes!"

"But you sent me, and then Jasmin, to find the artifacts because you wanted to protect the Clock. You thought the Jewels were dark forces stealing the artifacts." Jaffar looked at his father.

"Yes, that's all correct..." Khan trailed off.

"Jaffar," Uncle Idrees said cautiously as he finished pouring the tea. "Do you have a point?"

"Well," Jaffar continued, "here's what doesn't make sense. Mother heard that we were stealing the artifacts, so she sent the Jannah Jewels. But we only went after the artifacts after we heard the Jewels were pursuing them."

"After," Jaffar emphasized again. "That's why it doesn't make sense. Both you and mother sent out students to defend against... the students of the other, before they had even begun the chase? That is why it does not make sense."

"It is as if whoever told us both that the Clock was in danger knew that we both would send out students," Khan's eyes grew wide. "He knew we would both look for the artifacts because he pretended that someone was already stealing them. He lied so we would both come into the open."

"But why, Father?" Jaffar asked with a puzzled look on his face. "Why encourage both you and

Mother to send students to find the artifacts?"

"I understand now," Uncle Idrees said, shaking his head nervously. "We have all been tricked. Whoever did this, he is clever and thinks of the future. If Jaffar, Jasmin, and the Jannah Jewels fight, perhaps all of them will be too weak to fight in the Archery Battle and take the throne."

"And," Khan continued, "if any of them succeed in opening the Golden Clock, then whoever started this can try and steal the great secret. That will ensure he wins the Archery Battle."

"What a masterful plan!" Jaffar said in amazement. "But whose plan is it? And, what do we do to stop it?"

"For now, nothing." Khan argued. "For now, we pray that Jasmin has found your mother and convinced the Jannah Jewels to work with her. If we can all work together - the Jewels, your mother, you and Jasmin, all of us here in Fes - perhaps we can protect the Clock, the secret, and secure you or your sister the throne."

"We just have to hope that the Jannah Jewels

succeed in finding the artifact, and that no one stands in their way," Uncle Idrees said unconvincingly.

8

Danger

"First, however, we must eat," Sultan Razia said, "and there is a feast for all to enjoy!"

In the back of the Sultan's tent, two young men looked at each other. They wore dark heavy cloaks, one blue and one black. They both wore the hoods up over their heads, hiding their faces from anyone's view, "Hidayah will win the talent competition. The Jewels will get the quiver," said a deep voice from beneath the black hood.

"Do you think that the artifact is here?" his companion whispered.

"I'm sure of it. We must do something."

The two figures waited until the Sultan finished

talking to the girls and they left. Then the two men exited the back of the tent. They scurried to the main path and walked quickly toward the feasting tables.

"We do not know for sure that Hidayah will win the talent competition!" the man in blue exclaimed breathlessly as they raced.

"Oh come on! Are you crazy? She'll do her archery. She is so skilled, trained for years, trying to collect the artifacts! We must stop her at all costs!" the man in black responded.

"Ok, you're right," the man in blue reached his arm out and stopped his companion. The two ducked off the path to the edge of a crowd watching another strangely dressed man dancing with a monkey. They ignored the showman, instead turning to face the rows of feasting tables being set for the upcoming dinner.

The Sultan's table was at the front, on a strikingly decorated stand. The staff of the event were racing around, setting plates and fixing chairs.

"What can we do? We could sing and dance, perhaps?" The man in blue waved his hands excitedly.

"I'm sorry, have you lost your mind? Us? Perform? As talent? Against her archery? Oh my!" Laughter boomed from beneath the black hood.

In his mind, however, he was not laughing. It was imperative that he and his companion succeeded. The girls, working together, had stolen several of the artifacts. Now the Jewels were close to securing the quiver. Their boss was nowhere to be seen. Something had to be done. But performing in the competition? He knew there was no chance. And there was another problem at hand.

"And did you see Jasmin?" he continued.

His companion's head bobbed beneath his hood. "I did. I think she is being held hostage."

"She did not look in distress. And they did not look aggressive toward her."

"Indeed. Perhaps Jasmin is working with them in order to trick them?"

"It must be. Boss always said she was crafty. She is also a great archer. So she must be using the girls to get a spot in the talent competition. Then she plans to use her archery skills to be more impressive than Hidayah. I'm sure that once she wins the competition, she plans to escape with the artifact."

"But she would have to win. That's a gamble," the man in blue warned, "and we can't afford to risk it all on the archery skills of a woman we don't know! We need a plan! We need to steal it before the end of the competition!"

"There you go again, always with your silly ideas! There must be a dozen guards protecting it now while the feast and competitions are coming. No. We must wait! We must wait until the competition is over." The men squatted down and began tracing lines in the dirt with their fingers.

"Once someone has won the quiver, he or she will take it away with them. That is when we pounce - there will be fewer people around. We'll wait until he leaves the competition area. When it is late in the night, we steal the quiver quietly, from the shadows."

"Or when she leaves the competition. What if Jasmin wins?"

"Well," the man in black continued, "if Jasmin wins, she'll take the artifact back to her father, Khan. That will win his favor. Our boss can't allow that to happen. So we'll have to steal it from Jasmin if she is the winner. Still, that would be better than having to steal it from those Jewels. Four girls? Seems like it would be easier to steal the quiver from one girl than four, right?"

"So we have to make sure Hidayah doesn't win..." the young man trailed off. How do we make her lose, he wondered, when she is such a skilled archer? He had heard his boss describe her focus and discipline. And he remembered seeing her in action in the past; Hidayah's faith and belief in God's grace and her spiritual insight, were strong.

He looked around at the commotion, as people set cups out in front of each plate and began to set huge platters of meats and vegetables on the tables. Suddenly, his eyes lit up with inspiration.

"My friend... I know I always have the crazy ideas between us. But I have an idea that might work."

"Of course I will listen to your idea," the figure in black responded, "but I hope it is a good one, because we need to come up with something fast."

"Well, I was thinking… we know where Hidayah will be sitting. Surely we can slip among all these many workers. We can find her cup before the feast begins…"

"And slip her a potion! Yes! We can pour a potion in her pomegranate juice and when the Sultan makes her toast, Hidayah will drink it. Then, in just minutes, she will fall asleep," the man in black began rubbing his hands together. "Once asleep, she won't be able to compete, and then we'll wait to rob the winner."

"No, my friend," his companion said in a teasing tone, "now you are the one who is crazy! If Hidayah falls asleep, surely the Sultan will know that something is wrong. She is a smart ruler, with keen instincts, and she will know that someone has tampered with Hidayah's drink. Then the Sultan will cancel the competition and have her guards search all the guests. That could take days! And the quiver would still be heavily guarded."

"You see, we must mix that magical syrup I bought on our last journey with a bit of salt. Once Hidayah drinks it, her vision will change. She will see colors and shapes that are not really there, like the mirages of the desert."

The man in blue smiled and giggled. "She will make a fool of herself when she tries to shoot her bow and arrow. She will aim at phantoms and miss all her targets."

"And this will undermine her confidence. It will plant the seed in her mind that she is not a good archer. Then, when she competes in the Archery Battle, she will not trust her own head, hand or heart." The man in black lept to his feet. "Your plan, my friend, is pure art. I can practically see us returning with the quiver to our boss now!"

The two figures ran off to the side, looking at the tents along the edge of the dining area. The two men finally spotted a tent which had a steady stream of servers running in and out carrying heavy jugs of sweet juices.

The men snuck under the fabric of the tent in the

back, and wiggled into line. When they arrived at the front, they shrugged their shoulders.

"We dropped our jugs on the run back, and they cracked. We need new ones," the man in blue said after sliding up his hood and flashing a charming smile. The tired kitchen master sighed heavily, and then motioned to two jugs sitting on a side table. The pair picked up the jugs and filled them from the barrels of pomegranate and mango juices for the feast.

They exited the tent, ducking their heads as they passed into the late afternoon light and pulling their hoods forward to again hide their faces. They ran toward the table at the front of the feasting area, their jugs heavy with tangy juices.

9

Feast

Sultan Razia, flanked by her two guards, led the girls to the feasting area, still closed to the public. The servants were placing the last of the steaming hot platters of food on the tables, and pouring the last cups of juice.

The girls looked in awe at the hundreds of plates and pots of food. "Every year, I throw a grand feast in honor of my father. All my people are welcome," Sultan Razia explained, "and they may eat, no matter their wealth or class. We host feasts in all the major cities and out here, in the countryside, so that people from the cities and the jungles can all dine on the same day."

"Let me show you highlights from our menu today," the Sultan continued. "We have dishes from my empire and beyond, to celebrate our wonderful merchants and traders. Diversity is the spice of life!"

"We begin with a series of chicken, lamb and goat dishes from across my lands, from the Himalayas to the southern shores. Sauteed spinach, sweet cheese and cauliflower, and these," the Sultan motioned to thick, heavy flatbreads. "These are the naan. Beautiful flatbreads stuffed with garlic, peas, and onions."

"We put these chutneys on the breads - mango, mint, spicy peppers, and onions," the Sultan continued.

"Like peanut butter and jelly," Sara joked, "only made out of exotic flavors!"

"And of course, to tie it all together, fresh juice. Juice from pomegranates grown in my royal orchards, mixed with the sweet, crushed pulp of mangoes gathered from nearby jungles," Sultan Razia beamed with pride. She walked over to a layered dish smelling of nuts.

"Now, this dish here, Kanafeh, is a sweet cheese and pistachio dessert, soaked in sweet honey. It comes from traders we partner with who bring foods all the way from the Turkic and Byzantine lands in the far West." Sultan Razia pointed off into the sunset.

"Turkic?" Sara exclaimed, "Why, we've been to Istanbul! We've met the great Ottoman Sultan Muhammad and..."

"Sara, no!" Iman interrupted.

"Another Sultan! I love meeting Sultans! I have never heard of this Istanbul, but I'd love to meet this Sultan Ottoman..." Sultan Razia smiled with excitement.

"No, no," Hidayah leaned forward to block the Sultan's view of Sara. "She's just tired. We were in Constantinople. You must be friends with the Emperor there now, right?"

"Yes, Emperor John III," the Sultan said happily. "We both encourage trade along grand spice routes and the silk road."

"Sara!" Iman whispered quietly to her friend. "It's 1238 CE, remember? Istanbul hasn't happened yet!"

"Thank God, alhamdulillah, you are more clever than I am, Iman!" Sara exclaimed. "I didn't even think about that. Time travel sure is confusing."

"We are also serving a chicken and prune tagine stew with apricots. I have a cook who worked as a chef for the Sultan of Morocco in his youth," the Sultan bragged, "and he makes me the very best of flavors."

"He also buys almonds and saffron from Moroccan traders, to ensure the tastes are authentic." Sultan Razia smiled as she leaned forward to the platter, picked up a stewed prune and offered it to Jasmin.

Jasmin accepted the prune and put it in her mouth. The fruit exploded with hints of lemon and argan oil, and suddenly, Jasmin's eyes welled up with tears.

"Are you alright?" the Sultan asked, frowning with concern.

Jasmin smiled, "it tastes so much like home, it makes me miss my family. This tastes just like my Aunt Nur's stew. It is like a window back to home."

Jasmin's voice seemed so fragile and distant. The other girls lowered their heads, ashamed they had been so critical of Jasmin before.

"She has lost everything - her mother, her beliefs about her family, her purpose," Sara thought. "Perhaps I should not judge her."

Iman reflected on one of her mother's favorite Qur'anic passages: "Let them pardon and overlook. Would you not love for Allah to forgive you? Allah is Forgiving and Merciful." Iman realized that if she was not willing to be forgiving, then she was not being fair to ask Allah to forgive her when she was wrong.

"You know, all this talk about food... I'm surprised Jaide hasn't been trying to sneak a bite of every dish!" Hidayah exclaimed.

"Yeah, Jaide, this is the quietest you've ever been around food! What's the... Jaide?" Iman looked around the girls. "Hey, where's Jaide?"

The girls looked around frantically. Jaide, it appeared, had disappeared again. Suddenly, the Sultan let out a hearty laugh. She pointed to the table at the front of the room, sitting on a raised platform.

"Looks to me like she found our seats!"

The girls followed the Sultan through the maze of tables to the royal table. Crowds of dignitaries, merchants, artists and farmers began flooding into the feast area. The wild mess of colors and outfits added such energy to the party.

As the girls approached, Jaide blushed and slowly put a cup down on the table. "I... I thought we were coming right to our seats!"

"Jaide! The Sultan gave us a tour to show us all the foods from all over her empire!" Hidayah eyes widened and she spoke in a forced tone. "You don't want to be rude, do you?"

Jaide stood up very straight and tried to look serious. "Oh, Sultan Razia, I meant no disrespect. The smells were just so enticing. I could not help myself. And I... ummmm... I wanted to be sure each dish at your table was delicious enough for a Sultan."

The Sultan laughed. "And it looks like you had a bite of every dish here on our table!"

Jaide also laughed, "Yes! If you would like, I can serve you each dish and pour your juice!"

"Juice? Aren't all our drinks already poured?" the Sultan looked around to the staff with their giant jars of sweet nectar.

Jaide blushed again. "The food was so flavorful. I also tried the pomegranate juice. It was so bright and rich. I might have…"

The Sultan began laughing so hard that tears reached her eyes. "You drank all the juice at the table? All of it? Oh my friend! You are surely the most talented feaster I've ever seen!"

"Did she win the competition? She is very talented at feasting!" Iman teased Jaide. All the girls laughed, even Jasmin, and Jaide smiled warmly. Everyone took to their seats, and Sultan Razia motioned to her servants to bring over new jugs of pomegranate juice.

"Oh! Sultan! Can you ask them to bring over a new cup for Hidayah's seat?" Jaide requested. "The juice in her cup tasted sour and was thick. Her cup must've been dirty!"

"Of course! A new cup for Hidayah, and a feast for all!" The Sultan cheered and her subjects below all cheered as well. Everyone began passing platters and bowls around the tables, filling their plates with a mix of flavors, colors, and smells. The bounty of the Sultan's empire was vast.

The girls' plates became cluttered with Moroccan stew and Turkic pastry, and they tried the countless Indian chutneys on warm breads and crisps. For a little while, the girls enjoyed the trip, sharing stories, laughing and joking. They forgot the seriousness of their mission, and instead just enjoyed spending time with the Sultan.

But suddenly, Jaide started tapping on the table. "My sisters... something is wrong."

The girls turned and looked at their friend. "Perhaps it's your stomach, full of food and juice," Hidayah joked. "Maybe some patience would have been a good idea."

"Nooooooooooooo... woah... all the colors!" Jaide began staring at the ceiling, like she was seeing through it to the sky.

The Sultan jumped to her feet and told her guard to bring over her doctors. "We do not want to cause a scene, my friends, but I worry young Jaide has been poisoned. Let my doctors take her to the kitchen tent to check her health!"

"Poisoned?" Iman's voice broke with fear. The girls followed Jaide and the doctors to the kitchen tent, while the Sultan stayed at the table to ensure there was no commotion to scare the feasters.

The doctors looked at Jaide, and then talked in hushed tones. The girls sat and prayed together, for Jaide's well-being and good health. When the doctors motioned to them, the girls came forward to hear the news.

"Well," said the first doctor, "we have good news and bad news. The good news is that it is not a bad poison. She will have no permanent damage. Your friend will be fine." The girls sighed in relief. Their prayers had been answered. Hidayah said a quiet prayer immediately expressing her gratitude to God, something she learned the hard way back in Spain.

"But... the bad news is that she will see visions for the next few hours. Colors, shapes... these are tricks of the eyes," the second doctor explained.

"How did this happen?" Hidayah asked. The doctors shook their heads.

"We do not know. My best guess would be that she drank a poison, a bitter syrup of wormwood that causes these kinds of visions," the first doctor guessed.

The girls paused and thought. "Hidayah!" Jasmin yelled. "Your cup! Didn't Jaide say your cup of juice tasted wrong!"

"We never would have noticed the difference unless one person drank from every cup!" Sara argued. "Someone meant to poison Hidayah so she would see visions!"

"So that she would lose!" Jaide cut in. "So my feasting saved the day and woah, would you look at that unicorn in the corner over there!"

"Oh, Jaide, my friend," Iman could not help but laugh. "Indeed, you have saved the day!"

"Well, whomever didn't want Hidayah to win must have poisoned her," Sara concluded. "But who doesn't want Hidayah to win so badly that they would risk being caught?"

10

Hidden Talent

"Alright, Sara," Hidayah turned to her friend and smiled reassuringly. "You stay in the Sultan's booth with Jaide, and keep an eye on her. We'll compete. One of the three of us can surely win."

"Do I get a say? I say... woah... it's so colorful here! Look at all the outfits and the... woah!" Jaide exclaimed.

Sara handed her canteen to Jaide, who took a drink and passed it back. "We'd better get her up the stairs before she gets any more excited," Sara joked.

"No, no, look! This is why I'm excited!" Jaide waved her arm around frantically, until Iman grabbed it and held it still. Iman read the watch, then looked up.

"Oh no! According to this, we've only got 3 more hours to win the talent show and get back to the tree. One of us has to win!" Her voice was loud and scared.

"One of you guys can do it. We believe in you," Sara said confidently, and she followed a young strong woman who helped carry Jaide up to the Sultan's booth.

Jasmin, Iman, and Hidayah walked to the back of the tent, and then passed into the backstage area. There they were huddled behind a tent full of performers of all skin tones and fashions. The three girls sat together and began to pray that they would not get stage fright with such a large crowd watching.

Sara and Jaide reached the Sultan's booth, which was richly decorated with soft pillows and fluffy rugs. The Sultan sat in a chair carved from a fragrant sandalwood, and sipped from a cup of hot tea that smelled of lemon.

"I cannot wait to see the many talents of my

people. They have come from far and wide to share their skills."

As the girls looked down, the crowd grew quiet and the Master of Ceremonies introduced the talent competition. He explained the rules, and then he announced the grand prize would be awarded to the performer who pleased the Sultan the most.

The crowd cheered; Sara and Jaide along with it. They could not wait to start the show.

The first act was an entire family of Indians, each with a colorful sari and beautiful bracelets. They juggled a set of golden rings, first each alone, then between each other. The smallest daughter kept throwing up more rings. Before Jaide could believe it, the seven family members were juggling over fifty rings of various sizes, some looping around their arms like hula hoops.

When they finished, Jaide exclaimed, "it's like they spun spider webs around each other…"

"My goodness Jaide, " Sara exclaimed. "Drink some more water from my canteen. You're still seeing things."

"I suppose," Jaide agreed, taking a sip, "but if I didn't know better, I'd say Iman is down there dancing with some monkeys and... I'm not sure... maybe ferrets."

"What?" Sara turned around, and the Sultan shushed the girls.

"It's a mongoose, my sisters!" the Sultan explained. "A most important Indian creature. It is the only one fast and clever enough to hunt and kill a cobra. They protect people's homes, like good soldiers."

Below, half a dozen mongeese swayed gently to the sound of the music being played by a few drummers off stage. Iman and two monkeys were imitating each other in a comical dance battle. Each showed off their moves and made the audience laugh and cheer.

When Iman finished, she and the monkeys took a bow. One of the monkeys made a kissing motion up to the Sultan's box, and the Sultan laughed heartily. "So wonderful to see my people in touch with our beautiful natural world."

Next, a dashing young man walked on stage, wearing a bold emerald tunic and a heavy leather glove on his outstretched arm. Suddenly, a bright red parrot swooped into the room, over the heads of the crowd, and landed on his arm.

The man reached up and twirled his mustache between his fingers.

"Greetings, my friends. This is my partner, Arastoo. Say hello," the man's deep voice bellowed.

"SQWAK! Hello to the people! Salaam! Namaste! SQWAK!" The parrot's voice sounded strange, something none of the girls had heard before.

"My friends, we are Persian sailors, who have gathered pearls on the islands to the west, and collected corals from the reefs beyond the sea."

"SQWAK! He's the sailor!" the parrot whistled, "I'm the Captain!"

"Why, yes, I'm sure, Arastoo. And as Captain, do you have any advice for the people?"

As the audience watched, the young man had a back and forth conversation with the parrot, who had a very saucy sense of humor.

To the girls' amazement, the bird seemed just as smart as a person, and even responded to people in the crowd when they yelled. With a rousing song to close out their act, Arastoo and his human friend took their bow and a singing act took the stage.

Jaide turned to the Sultan, "Pardon me, Master, but I would love to know: how will you determine the person who wins this talent competition?"

"Well,' Sultan Razia responded, "anyone can perfect a performance for a crowd. But someone who teaches me something, that it a true talent. Perhaps I will learn something about beauty, or truth. Perhaps I will learn a new way to shoot an arrow, or a new way to practice meditation."

"But whatever I learn, if it helps me be a better leader, it is a valuable lesson. Teaching a Sultan is a powerful talent." The Sultan nodded her head, and Jaide smiled in agreement.

"Jaide, look, it's Jasmin!" Sara exclaimed.

As the girls looked to the stage, Jasmin marched on proudly. She thought of all the times she and her brother had put on little talent shows for their old friends Moe and Slim, and Jasmin pretended that there was only a small audience of friends rather than a massive crowd watching eagerly.

"Ladies and gentlemen, I'm here to show you what a young girl can do with a bow and arrow... blindfolded! Can I get a volunteer from the audience?" Jasmin said confidently.

She picked a young boy from the crowd who was waving his hand wildly in the air. He hopped onto the stage, holding a bright red pomegranate. She told him to stand against the side of the stage, and Jasmin placed the pomegranate onto his head.

Then she tied a scarf around her eyes, tucking it into her headscarf to be sure she couldn't see anything. The crowd grew quiet, to allow Jasmin to focus.

"Allah, be my guide. May this arrow travel straight and true." Jasmin took a deep breath, and settled her focus, remembering the scene and listening to her senses.

Jasmin drew her bow, called out, "in sha Allah!"

and released the arrow. She heard a whipping sound as the arrow zipped through the air. Then, the crowd gasped as she heard a thick thud, then two bumps on the floor.

She ripped off the blindfold to see the boy, smiling, pointing to the two halves of pomegranate on the floor at his sides. Jasmin had split it right down the middle. The crowd cheered triumphantly. Jasmin bowed, and handed the two halves of the pomegranate to the boy, to snack on during the rest of the competition.

"Wow, that was very exciting!" the Sultan cheered. "Did you see her focus and faith? It helped her see when her eyes could not. That is a difficult skill to master."

"What a lovely display!" Jaide chimed. "But I think Hidayah's will be better. She trained with Sensei Elle!"

"Well, so did Jasmin…" Sara remarked, shaking her head in confusion. How was she supposed to know Sensei Elle was Jasmin's mother? What did the whole mission mean now? And Jasmin's archery skills were very impressive - would she be able to beat Hidayah in the Archery Battle if they managed to open the Golden Clock?

"I see bouncing children!" Jaide cheered.

"Jaide, that's ridiculous! Children aren't balls! They don't bounce!"

"But look!" Jaide was pointing down to the stage, and Sara couldn't believe her eyes. Below, half a dozen small children were performing a tumbling act. Like mini-gymnasts, they flipped and rolled over the stage, springing up and down like bouncing balls.

The crowd clapped to the rhythm of the children's dancing. The boys and girls locked into pyramid shapes, and dancing in time together to make fun shapes and amuse the audience.

As the clapping continued, the children performed some fantastic jumps and somersaults, fearlessly leaping through the air. For their finale, the kids climbed on top of each other into the shape of a pyramid, with big smiles and happy eyes greeting the Sultan.

Behind the stage, Jasmin was putting away

her bow and arrows, when she noticed Hidayah stretching her bow in preparation for her performance. Suddenly, a thought occurred to Jasmin. "Hidayah, wait!"

11

Diversity

Jasmin ran up to Hidayah and walked with her as she prepared to go on stage. "I was thinking - I just did a feat of archery. And I looked at the Sultan, and she did not seem very impressed. If you also do archery…"

"…she may not choose either of us to win," Hidayah responded. "I must perform some other talent."

"Yes," Jasmin said. "What will you do?"

"I… this is so sudden." Hidayah's head felt like it was spinning. "I wish Jaide were able to ride her skateboard… Or Sensei Elle was here to tell me what to do."

"Just pray. Allah will show you the way." Jasmin knew that Hidayah had the most spiritual insight out of the Jannah Jewels. If anyone could hear Allah's advice in this emergency, it would be her.

She cleared her mind, and tried to pray to Allah for help. She hoped she would sense what to do. When her name was finally called in what seemed like an eternity, she knew that it was time to act.

Hidayah took a deep breath. Suddenly, she felt a slip of paper in her hand. Somehow, when her mind was deep in thought, her hand had reached into her pocket, and pulled out the slip of paper the Masters had handed her before they left.

"We have created you from male and female

and made you peoples and tribes

that you may know one another."

Hidayah stepped on stage, and there were hundreds of faces staring up at her. She used the techniques Sensei Elle taught her to clear her mind and calm her heart. She reflected on the passage on the paper, and in the clearness of her mind, she finally spoke.

"I come to you, people of the empire, to reflect on the words of the Qur'an. You are a living example of the wisdom of Allah. He said to us all: We have created you from male and female and made you peoples and tribes that you may know one another."

"There is such wisdom in this simple statement. This festival has been an opportunity for men and women of the many peoples and tribes of Sultan Razia's empire to come together to live out the words of Allah - to know one another."

"In this empire, I see men and women working together to make a better world. A woman Sultan leads with strength and grace. In many parts of the world, throughout the history of mankind, we see societies afraid of women leaders. Yet, as Allah reminds us, males and females must all work in unison to make society great for all of us."

"At this festival, I saw people from across the empire sharing their lives. They were singing, dancing, and eating together. They were discussing ideas, reading the Qur'an, debating art and philosophy. They were trading goods and having fun. By knowing one another, they made something better."

"On those feasting tables sat the foods and cultures of many people. The Sultan was proud of that food. Vegetables and fruits raised by the hands of her own people. Spices picked, animals raised, all harvested by her people. These dishes are the result of generations of hard working women and men across her empire. The earth beneath all our feet provides for all these peoples and tribes."

"And in this talent show, we have seen so many different skills and talents. By sharing our knowledge and skills, we can become a better show, and a stronger team." Hidayah looked off stage to Jasmin. "By learning more about each other, we learn more about ourselves."

"This is the legacy of Sultan Razia," Hidayah concluded. "Historians will look back on these days and applaud how talented we all are by being so diverse, by listening to Allah's plan. When men and women share knowledge, and diverse peoples live together in peace, life is better for all."

"My people," the Sultan rose to her feet and the crowd turned to face her booming voice. "I have seen enough! The young Hidayah has demonstrated a great talent. Her words have reached my heart, and shown me a true understanding of my belief as a Sultan."

"This young girl sees the truth that Allah teaches us, and the truth that I have always used as the foundation of our empire.

We have created you from male and female

and made you peoples and tribes

that you may know one another."

"As a female Sultan, I am living proof that Allah has made both men and women that we might learn from each other and make our world a better place. These performers from across my empire, men, women, and children of talent, are proof of that."

"Hidayah's speech and reflection on the Qur'an showed us all the deeper meaning in this passage," Sultan Razia concluded. "For someone so young to show us all Allah's wisdom, and for someone so young to have such an understanding of our people within the course of history... Truly, she is the most talented here today."

"So with that," the Sultan cheered, "here is the prize!" She raised her hand to the stage, where the Master of Ceremonies brought out the stunning silver quiver.

Across the quiver were beautiful scenes of animals from India - elephants, tigers, mongeese, and monkeys. "Our empire is a peaceful garden full of all Allah's creatures and peoples, that we may know one another!" Sultan Razia cheered.

Hidayah stepped forward and took the silver quiver to the applause of the crowd. Jasmin and Iman joined Hidayah on stage and the three waved to Jaide and Sara in the Sultan's box.

12

Teamwork

"Jewels, we have to get going! Remember Jaide's watch? We only have half an hour left and we must run all the way back to the mango tree!" Hidayah's voice betrayed her, and the other girls could hear how worried she was. That mango tree was very far away.

"Well, my talented friend," the Sultan's voice sprang to life. "I think I know where you can catch a ride. Meet me out front of the tent." Sultan Razia turned and led Jaide and Sara down the small set of stairs to the ground level of the tent. The guards led them quickly through the crowd to the front of the tent. Just as they approached, Iman and Jasmin, both hugging Hidayah who carried her new prize, came racing to the tent flap. As the doorman lifted the massive tent flap with a pole, the girls smiled to see a familiar face.

Haati winked at Iman, and the Sultan gestured to the guards to begin helping the Jewels and Jasmin up onto the silver pillow on the back of the large elephant. "Remember always to work together, no matter your differences," the Sultan exclaimed. "And make sure Jaide stays away from pomegranate juice for a while!"

As the Sultan waved to the girls, Haati turned and trotted away from the tent, making his way quickly along the widest routes throughout the festival. Soon he was back on the road along the jungle, moving at a pace surprising for an elephant. The girls held tight onto the pillow, trying not to fly off the bouncing behind of the elephant.

With all the commotion, the girls failed to notice two dark, hooded figures slip out of the feast tent just after them. The figures began to chase Haati on foot, but as the elephant raced up the first hill, the two figures stopped and stomped their feet in frustration.

"Ladies, I must ask," Iman yelled as she bounced precariously on the pillow. "How are we supposed to find the mango tree on the edge of the jungle? How will we know which one it is?"

"Oh! Me! Me me me!!!" Jaide yelled out excitedly. "I remember the mango tree! I climbed it, and spent time at the top. I remember what the mangos look like up there. And since they are bright yellow and red, I'll spot them easily with my special vision!"

Jasmin chimed in, "Well, Jaide, I don't know if you have special visions so much as mirages..."

"Well, we've got less than 2 minutes on the watch, so we have to do something! And I think I see the tree top from up here! Haati," Jaide yelled as she pointed, "take us to that tree!"

Haati stopped in front of the tree, and knelt to the ground. The girls slid off his back, and ran over to the tree. Iman stopped for a brief moment and rested her hand on the elephant's head, between his eyes.

"Peoples and tribes," he says, "that we may

know one another."

"Goodbye, my friend."

"Iman!!! We've got to go!" Sara's voice was full of urgency.

Iman ran forward and caught up with the girls at the base of the tree. They counted down from three, and then pushed against the tree trunk together. It buckled under their weight, and gave way. When they reached the bottom, the five girls locked hands and recited in unison, "Bismillah hir Rahman nir Raheem!"

The girls found themselves inside the familiar tree, and walked up to the Golden Clock. Hidayah lifted the silver quiver for all to see. Wrapped around it, sculpted beautifully in the silver, were scenes of dancers, acrobats, animals, and feasters, all wearing different costumes.

"We must celebrate each other's cultures to gain the wisdom Allah hopes for us. This quiver represents that diversity." Hidayah wondered if its weightiness was from its meaning or just the silver.

She pushed the quiver into the 10 o'clock slot,

and it clicked neatly. The room seemed to grow a little brighter as the clock neared completion.

"So we hope you've had some time to think about your teamwork," Sensei Elle's voice rang from the dark shadows of the room. The girls turned to see the Masters all standing behind them, smiling.

"Mother! We found the quiver! And a female Sultan!" Jasmin had truly enjoyed her time with her newfound friends.

"And an elephant!" Iman exclaimed, "I'll never forget him! And I bet he'll never forget me!"

"Most importantly, we learned that we need to each bring our skills to the team in order to succeed," Hidayah smiled. "And we couldn't have done it without Jasmin."

"And did you find wisdom in the passage from the Qur'an?" the Master Archer asked.

"Yes. The Sultan was a woman leader, showing that both men and women are needed for a peaceful world," Jasmin responded.

"And at the festival," Iman noted, "we saw people

and animals from many different lands, sharing languages and ideas. It brought understanding and happiness."

Sara chimed in, "The talent competition also helped us see that, even if we come from different backgrounds, we can all be amazed or impressed or amused by the same skills."

"Ok, hey! Over here!" Jaide waved her hand frantically. "I also learned an important lesson. I learned to look before I drink," the girls looked at each other and giggled, smiling. "And not be impatient with pomegranate juice. I think I'm still seeing colors from that poisoned cup!"

"Wait, Jaide!" The Master Artist looked at her student with great concern. "You drank poison?"

"No, I'm fine. It was a strange potion that made me see mirages," Jaide assured her mentor. "I feel fine now!"

"But... who tried to poison you?" Sensei Elle questioned in a worried tone.

The girls looked at each other, thinking back through everything that had happened.

"I don't…" Hidayah trailed off.

Jasmin finished her thought, "…we don't know!"

Don't miss the next Jannah Jewels book!

Who were the hooded men who tried to poison Hidayah and sabotage the talent competition? Who are the two hooded men working for? Is Jasmin really helping the Jannah Jewels or is it just a trick? Will the Jannah Jewels be able to find the last two artifacts to reveal the secret in the Golden Clock before time runs out?

Find out in Book 11 of the next Jannah Jewels Adventure Series, "Evidence in Egypt."

Find out more about the eleventh book by visiting our website at www.JannahJewels.com

Glossary

Ambergris: used in perfumery

Biodegradable: capable of decaying through the action of living organisms

Bismillah hir Rahman nir Raheem: In the Name Of God, The Most Merciful, The Most Compassionate

Delhi Sultanate: a Muslim kingdom based mostly in Delhi that stretched over large parts of the Indian subcontinent for 320 years (1206–1526)

In sha Allah: Arabic language expression for "God willing" or "if God wills"

Jumu'ah: congregational prayer that Muslims hold every Friday

Kanafeh: a sweet cheese and pistachio dessert, soaked in sweet honey

Mongoose: a small carnivorous mammal with a long body and tail and a grizzled or banded coat, native to Africa and Asia.

Nimantran: an invitation to a specific event that is taking place

Quiver: a case for arrows

Salaam: Peace

Sultana: an Islamic title and a feminine form of the word sultan. This term has been legally used for some Muslim women monarchs

Tagine: a North African stew of spiced meat and vegetables prepared by slow cooking in a shallow earthenware cooking dish with a tall, conical lid.

SARA

To find out more about our other books,

go to:

www.JannahJewels.com

Made in the USA
Columbia, SC
29 April 2018